THE GRIEF EATER

The Grief Eater

A collection of short stories

by

DEIRDRE FAGAN

BOOKS

Adelaide Books
New York / Lisbon
2020

THE GRIEF EATER
A collection of short stories
By Deirdre Fagan

Copyright ©Deirdre Fagan
Cover design © 2020 Adelaide Books

Published by Adelaide Books, New York / Lisbon
adelaidebooks.org
Editor-in-Chief
Stevan V. Nikolic

For any information, please address Adelaide Books
at info@adelaidebooks.org
or write to:
Adelaide Books
244 Fifth Ave. Suite D27
New York, NY, 10001

ISBN: 978-1-953510-63-1

Printed in the United States of America

In memory of my mother, Maureen, my father, Frank,

my eldest brother, Paul, my middle brother, Sean,

lost friends and lost loves, and for all those

whom have ever had to eat their own or another's grief.

Acknowledgments

I am grateful to the editors of the journals where these stories first appeared and to the members of my Illinois writing circle for offering feedback and suggestions on early drafts. I am thankful for the various professional and financial support of the English, Literature, and World Languages Department, the College of Arts & Sciences, and the Faculty Center for Teaching and Learning at Ferris State University. I also very much appreciate the confidence of The Popular Culture Association for offering opportunities to read a number of these stories at conferences. I extend deep gratitude to cover artist Dayan Moore. Thanks also to dear friends and colleagues who believed in these stories, and especially my husband, Dave, my late husband, Bob, and my children Maeve and Liam for always believing in me.

Contents

The thing is…

We are all characters,
characters in a play,
a play of our own making.

And we can change the set,
and the lights,
and the stage.

Wear make-up,
or not.
Hell, even a wig.

We can even alter
our character,
or play several at once.

But the music—
so little of that is in our control.

And the audience,
the one we imagine and prepare for,
rarely arrives.

The one in the front, center,
is the one who came—
not always the one we want.

And when the tickets sell,
it's often not for the right reasons,
whatever they are, but most certainly the wrong,
which we usually know, or can at least imagine most clearly.

The marquee always gets it wrong.
It's salacious, and we are all bones, atoms,
and other things not illuminated by lights.

So the show goes,
sometimes with tap dancing,
and we sing.

Trespassing

It was about 11 a.m. when I finally put a load of wash in. And when I got down to the laundry area, I just froze. I smelled a man—that musky, sweaty sort of smell that a man gets when he hasn't showered for a couple of days. You know the smell. I started moving some boxes around, opening doors, lifting the toilet seat in the basement bathroom, looking for where the smell was coming from, but I just knew this was no dead mouse. I've smelled dead things before. This was a raw scent. This was most definitely sweat. After a while I found myself just standing there, feeling panicked, afraid to move, realizing, and thinking, *Where is he? How did he get in?* Then I started sniffing the walls, but suddenly the scent disappeared. I couldn't smell it anymore, and now I wasn't even sure what I'd initially smelled. Maybe it was all in my imagination, y'know?

But the next day I found myself going down to the basement to find the smell because I really didn't think it was all in my mind. I mean, I have a good sense of smell. I'm one of those people. Every time I was pregnant it was ridiculous. I could barely be in the world with other people, because I could smell EVERYTHING. So I got down to the basement and I smelled it, right where I had before. It was a man; I just knew it. It was not something dead. But I couldn't figure out where it was coming from. This second time I was less freaked out, though. At first I thought if there was someone in the house he meant to harm me, but at this point I'd been in the house alone for two days in a row and, *shh*, I was even masturbating, *twice*, yikes, and so far so good. If there was a killer in the house, you'd think he would have taken his opportunity while he had it, right?

So then I went upstairs with a batch of clothes and I was sitting in the living room folding when I pulled out a pair of Fruit of the Loom green briefs. A shiver ran through me again like it did the day before when I had first smelled the smell.

Jeff does not wear green briefs. Jeff wears black boxer briefs only. *What are these doing in here?* I thought to myself. *Is Jeff wearing different underwear with some other woman? Is he having an affair with a* man? *Or is the man in the basement putting his laundry in with ours?* I know, I know, I sounded crazy even to myself, especially with that last one—"the man in the basement." That's what he had become in my mind at this point. *What's the matter with me?* I thought. *I've been at home for too long. Too much coffee, too many novels, too much time folding laundry and cleaning toilets. Something is going wrong with my head.* So, I picked up the phone and called Jeff, and I got his voicemail AGAIN, right away. I threw the phone across the room, yelled "*Bastard!*" and burst into tears. He was clearly cheating on me.

The next few weeks passed with me not really thinking about the man in the basement much, except when I was doing the laundry and folding more briefs and then t-shirts and socks that I swore weren't Jeff's. And then I got the idea to start placing the clothes on the washing machine at night, and in the morning, they were always gone! And I was afraid to talk about it, so I just didn't. I assumed Jeff was shopping with some little mistress and buying new things, and then taking the folded items to work with him each day to change, and I didn't really want to know what the truth was, so I didn't say anything at all to Jeff. *Maybe he feels less guilty about cheating on me in colored briefs*, I thought to myself. But then the smell didn't go away in the basement. I started to figure it really was something dead after all, or some sort of old wood smell I didn't know about, and I left it at that. A guy would have turned up by now, right?

And then our electric bill came and it had gone up by nearly $30.00! And we hadn't done anything differently (except for maybe the extra socks and underwear in the wash). We were even on vacation for three weeks before the smell, so I just couldn't figure it out. I decided I should talk to Jeff about the smell, but after he was so dismissive in our conversation about it, laughing at my crazy imagination, I became more convinced that there was another man in the house, even if that man did leave me alone while I was masturbating.

So, I kept doing the laundry and it all kept disappearing! Then about another week later, one of the kids reported there was a man on the front steps. I went out to see who he was, and guess what? I found this very drunk guy of about sixty sitting on our stoop with his head in his hands in despair.

Just a second. I need to take a drink.

Okay. So I'm out on the stoop and the man is staring at his shoes, sort of mumbling to himself, and I feel worse and worse looking at him. I wonder why he has had so much to drink so early and where he was coming from when he decided to sit down. I knew Jeff would tell me I was "off my rocker" for doing this, but I brought him into our kitchen anyway. He came willingly, mumbling something incoherent.

Not everyone is a criminal, y'know?

So, I got the man a cup of coffee and two pieces of toasted rye bread right here at this table, and he ate the bread quickly but only sipped at the coffee.

Do you want more coffee? No? Okay.

Well, he looked very tired, but I knew I couldn't let him lie down. Jeff was going to be home soon, like he is today. What time is it, Matthew? 6:14? Wow, it's later than I thought. The kids will be dropped off soon, too.

That day it was about 5:30 when I glanced up at the clock, and I figured that I should make sure he was gone by 6:00. Jeff said that he'd be home right after work, like tonight. So, after about fifteen minutes of letting him just sit there quietly with his head down, I explained he was going to have to leave soon. There was an eerie silence and I was beginning to wonder what I had done by bringing him inside, and how I was going to get him back out the door without being rude, when he suddenly shoved his chair back, steadied himself by leaning his full body weight on the table right where you are now, got up, and then stumbled around the table, in the opposite direction of the door. I was beginning to panic again, you know, for a different reason. I was afraid he was going to fall and bump his head, and then I'd have to explain what this passed out man was doing on the kitchen floor when Jeff got home, but I managed to stutter out, "Sir, sir, the back door is this way. Do you want me to help you?" but he didn't seem to hear me. I guess the coffee and bread hadn't done much good! He tripped a bit on one of his feet, then reached for the basement door, and pulled it open. That surprised me. "Sir, that's not the way out, Sir, let me help you go this way," I said. But he mumbled something I couldn't make out again and went down into the basement, leaving the door open behind him. *It was him!* You knew that's where I was going with this, right?

The next day I wondered if I should just do the laundry like always, or if I should start looking for him. I was worried maybe I'd startle him, or maybe he would turn violent. I figured I should just assume he'd remember me from the day before. He couldn't have been that drunk, right? So I decided to bring him a cup of coffee. I thought of calling the police, but didn't. I decided to just act like we were friends.

The next morning, I was nervously picking at my shirt as the coffee brewed, and Jeff noticed. He was like, "Crystal, what's the matter with you?" but I didn't trust him enough to tell him anymore. I just couldn't wait for him to get out the door so I could go to the basement.

After practically shoving Jeff out the door, I poured two cups and walked quietly downstairs. When I got to the bottom, I set both cups on the washing machine and listened, and then I heard him say behind me, "Good morning, Crystal, and thank you." I was startled, you can bet I was, but I tried not to show it, "Hello?" I said a bit hesitantly as I swiveled around. I mean, he knew my name. "I'm sorry about yesterday, I'm sorry about everything, my name is Jim," he said and shook my hand very formally. I playfully said, "Welcome to our house?" With a question mark. Like that. Just like that. Well, he took a few steps back and suddenly stuttered, "I'm sorry, I'm really sorry, I'm, I'm so so sorry," and began sobbing into his hands like he was ashamed. I wasn't really sure what to do—I instinctually hug people when they begin crying—but I didn't want to do that, that would be like my hugging you right now, and so I went and got the coffee cups off of the washer and offered him one. "Here, why don't we go upstairs and have some coffee?" I asked. He pulled himself together and then we came up here.

Are you sure you don't want more coffee?

So, I put some toast in the toaster and Jim just began rambling. "I used to live in this house. It was a home for boys. I lived here when I was small. Four of us shared one of the rooms upstairs. Your room...." "Your room" sure took me by surprise and then I remembered the other day and wondered if he saw me. If he knew. I was becoming suddenly uncomfortable again.

"...I once set this kitchen on fire, by accident...." *Fire? Oh shit*, I thought. At this point I really wasn't sure if I should be in the house alone with him. He wasn't like you.

Jim said, "...It was a grease fire. I was cooking french fries...I painted that porch for punishment once...the place has changed since I lived here, there's been some renovations, but I could easily find my way around, and I know that basement...boy did we play in that basement...I was about Abby's age when I lived here...."

Yeah, just like that, all strung together. Then, Jim's expression changed. I was wondering if mine had, too, and if so, how to hide it. Sometimes you can't hide what you are feeling, like if you are tense...or scared.

Then Jim said, "My granddaughter was taken." I thought, *Taken? Oh my god.* And then he said she was taken from the church parking lot down the street. "Abby. Abby was eight," he said. He said he was "watching" Abby. Said he "thought she was old enough," and that she could go half a block away by herself. That he "told her not to talk to strangers." I felt so sorry for him. It was so sad.

And guess what? Despite myself, I put my hand on Jim's shoulder, like this. And then he turned toward me. Yeah, like that. And he said, "She's been gone for over a year. They found her remains. It's all my fault." And then he started choking out sounds I shouldn't have been hearing. I was embarrassed. I felt like an intruder. I pulled my hand back at the word "remains." Like this.

I felt like I was going to throw up. I started shaking and my eyes began to blur. I had this sudden urge to run, but I was in my house. "It is my house," I thought. Just then that toaster began smoking and the smoke alarm went off, and he got up from the table and went to the bathroom. It was all so fast. I turned the alarm off and threw out the toast, and while I was standing here alone, I remembered hearing the story. Only, it didn't happen a year ago. It was more like several months. Remember? It happened a little while before Jeff and I went on vacation, a few months before. But I didn't remember hearing that they had found the girl, or what they thought happened, had you? I only knew that she had gone missing.

So I was here in the kitchen beginning to wonder about Jim. It seemed like he'd been in the bathroom a long time.

I knocked on the door, "Jim?" "Jim?" "Are you okay?" On the third knock, Jim yanked the door open. "I'm fine," he said, and he sounded like Jeff all of a sudden. Dismissive. But he looked different. Not at all like Jeff. Empty. Angry. I wasn't sure how to respond, but I had that shiver up my spine again. Gosh. I almost feel it right now. Has it gotten cold in here? Anyway, I felt a sudden need to protect myself. I was in a serious situation and I was not entirely sure how I had gotten there.

I became forceful as I backed away, and I said, like this, "Then I think we need to talk about what you are going to do."

And, oh my god, out of nowhere Jim shouted, "What I'M going to do?! What do you mean what I'M going to do?! I'M not going to do anything, YOU are." And lunged at me. My stomach emptied as the coffee traveled up my throat. I almost feel it again now.

I thought he was nice.

I am not sure what happened next but I woke up in the basement. Right downstairs. I was sore all over, which I later found out was from being shoved down the stairs. I'm better now. But guess what? He was picked up the next afternoon and charged with trespassing and assault. A woman about six blocks away saw him entering *her* basement through *her* bulkhead cellar door. As it turns out, the story he had told me was true. He was Abby's grandfather. And Abby's remains *had* been found, and it was all over the local news, but I don't watch the news. It's just too real, you know? And things like that don't usually happen here anyway.

I guess he just sort of lost it. I don't know. I felt sorry for him. I really did. I still do. But you know what? Now that he's locked up, I actually feel pretty good about it. And I know I'm so much safer now. We all are. It's like they say, it's like this was all supposed to happen. You know what I mean? Like it's all part of a larger plan. Like his showing up here was meant to be. Like it's all part of learning to forgive people for things. Or forgive ourselves. Or something.

Everything sure does happen for a reason, Matthew. It sure does, don't you agree? Like you, here, now. But I shouldn't really be rambling like this. You are so sweet, just to come in, and sit there, and listen to me go on and on about my life and my problems. So different from my Jeff.

Now where did you say you are from again? And what was it you were saying before, about what kind of work you were hoping to get when you knocked? Raking some leaves? I'm sure we can come up with something. You really are sweet to put up with me this afternoon. You really are. Here, let me get you another cup of coffee before you go.

By Sweater

There once was a boy who was a good boy most of the time, who on one particular occasion was not quite so good. Officers picked him up for his not-so-goodness on a particularly not-so-good night. They didn't arrest him; they decided to hold him in a cell instead. Overnight. Until he was right. Until he was fit.

The boy who was usually good was not quite himself, and yet he was very much himself.

They took the boy to the station where they would book him without throwing the book at him.

The boy was not behaving, not keeping his mouth shut. He continued to shout and flail about, to grab and to hit.

The boy was put in a cell but it did not quiet his tongue.

The boy's father, a good father most of the time but not all the time, called the station to find his son.

The boy who was not quite so good on this particular occasion had made the officers who were often not good even less good than they were most often.

An arm of the law opened the cell and grabbed the boy about the neck instead of about the tongue and squeezed hard for too long. The squeezing quieted the boy's tongue. The boy did not flail, shout, or hit. The boy hung limp. Too limp for a living boy.

The father who called the police to find his son waited on a phone line listening to silence. His tongue was quiet as he poised it for speech.

The silence was terminal. His speech, belated.

The boy, the father was told, had hung himself with his sweater in the jail cell.

The autopsy report confirmed that the bruises along the neck were caused by strangulation.

A sweater with long sleeves perhaps, a sweater strong enough to hold a 140lb. boy about the neck and suspended in air long enough to suffocate.

A sweater perhaps, or long sleeves attached to a uniform, attached to a man, who was also a boy, who also had a father, whose father did not have to wait on a phone line for terminal instructions.

A boy in a uniform who would live knowing he had in one report been described as a sweater.

A father left to live not with someone else's injustice but with what sorts of injustices he would have time to imagine had been his own and had caused his good boy most of the time to take his life on one particularly not good night.

And a boy no longer in a sweater who had died not by his own hands but by someone else's, not bare-chested but in the sweater that would later be described as a weapon.

A particularly not good night and yet all too typical.

Yo-Yo

I.

I used to sit and think about ways to do it. I did. Which was the easiest. Which was the least painful. Which was the quickest. Which was a surefire way to get the job done. And then one day my father did it, and I didn't think about doing it anymore. I began instead to think about reasons why people do it. But one day I realized that the reasons are endless, and the ways almost unlimited. So now I think about other things. Like which is the best way to eat a pomegranate or why men and women cohabitate.

I know, they don't appear related, but if you think about it maybe you'll understand what I mean. The point is that there are plenty of things to think about other than killing yourself.

I remember this time I walked past a man on the street. He wasn't walking; he was just on the street. He was holding a sign. We've all seen them before, the ones that ask for a job, or a place to sleep, or money. Usually we try not to think about it. But that day I got to thinking. At one time this man was a tiny little baby. And then one day he wasn't. And then one day he was like this. And then I said to myself, how does that happen? But I didn't have any answer. How do we get from point A to point B, I asked? But I didn't know, so I started thinking about that and I've been thinking about it ever since.

II.

Last week I spent a night with a woman. She was very beautiful. She had great big brown eyes and soft skin.

I had never spent the entire night holding a woman before. Holding her was like holding a delicate opalescent moth, the sort you want to put into a glass jar and keep. That night I discovered that being held by a woman is very different from being held by a man. Women smell different and they sleep different but most of all they feel different; they can be held and they can hold you in a way a man just can't. Women sort of melt into women. Men have a different effect: women sort of *mold* into them. Men simply aren't palpable in the way women are. Y'know when you get up from a chair and slowly the indentation from where you were sitting returns to its original shape? When women are with men it's sort of like that. Women can bounce back to the way they were before a man held them but while they're being held they just mold right into them. With two women it's different—it's like trying to separate melted ice from water.

Relationships between the sexes are like that. You meet men, some of them interesting, all of them different. You think that each one makes you feel better than the last. All of them seem to like the strangest things about you, all the things you've spent your entire life hiding. The way you blow your nose or the funny sounds you make while you're sleeping. You eventually start spending all of your time with one of these men, and inevitably you begin to tell him all about the things that happened in your childhood. Like the first time you got stung by a bumble bee, or the time you made snow angels until you got frostbite, or the time your mother hit you in the face so hard you couldn't go to school. This man, apparently different from the rest, is the one you make a connection with. You like his sense of humor, his quirky smile, his skinny toes. You desperately want to be with him. That's when you begin to mold into him.

You start spending all of your time with him and you decide that you don't want ever to be without him. He thinks he doesn't want ever to be without you either, so you move in together. At least that was the way it happened when I first met Ben. I was going through a really rough time. It was after my father did it and just after I stopped thinking about doing it myself. I had lost faith in just about everything. I thought: it doesn't matter if we even get to point B; might as well quit while you're ahead. But that was before I met Ben.

III.

I met Ben on the street. It was springtime. He was walking; I wasn't. He looks like one of those guys who is totally unapproachable, the kind who holds his head so high you wonder how he can get enough air. But it turns out he isn't. In fact, we got tangled up at a time when I was the one who was pretty much unapproachable.

I have this thing for yo-yos. I've collected them since I was about thirteen. I don't know what it is about them exactly; maybe it has something to do with their freedom of motion or the way they just keep going up and down, the continuity of it, the lack of any points, A or B. Yo-yos don't always have it good, though. Sometimes the string gets really loose and then you have to spend time mending the yo-yo—wrapping the string back around its body.

My interest in yo-yos happened to me because of puberty. The transformation from tomboy to woman was difficult for me. I guess I wanted to hold on to something childlike, something playful. So I started collecting yo-yos, all different shapes and colors. I had glow-in-the-dark yo-yos, yo-yos that ran on batteries, some shaped like butterflies, some that danced crazily. I guess you could say I became sort of addicted to them. Everybody has a crutch; I had yo-yos. When I became a woman I continued to collect them, but by then I guess you could say they were more of an affliction than a preoccupation.

The day I met Ben I really had an urge to walk the dog. Not a real dog. The kind of dog you walk with a yo-yo. It's the dog that comes right on back to you—that trick where you sort of roll the yo-yo out and back it comes. So the day I met Ben I was standing on the corner outside this drug store walking the dog. Ben was walking down the street quickly and I didn't see him coming. I rolled out my yo-yo and what came back was Ben with his legs tangled in a nasty mess of yo-yo string. It was a very awkward situation. Perfect stranger meets perfect stranger in yo-yo string accident—not exactly the ideal beginning for a hot and steamy romance.

Ben and I moved in together six months to the day after the accident. Ben always referred to our first meeting as "the accident" (which demonstrated how little experience Ben had with accidents). His reference came to have more meaning than it did initially.

Ben came with everything: good looks, education, a shower curtain, a crock-pot, matching socks.... I came with a bag full of all kinds of yo-yos. The day we moved into the apartment over the toy store Ben and I made love in every room and on every freestanding appliance: the washer and dryer, the little refrigerator, the dishwasher. Ben said to me: "This is it, this is what life is about. I want to wake with you every morning and go to bed with you every night. I want to skinny-dip in our neighbor's backyard pool on weekends and maybe someday own a gas grill. I want to grow old with you and watch as the beautiful little laugh lines deepen around your mouth." I said I wanted to put crayons in the bathroom and let guests draw on the walls.

Living with Ben was wonderful. We did everything the way it should be done. We cleaned together, ate together, slept together, read together, and knew how to leave each other alone. Loneliness is the best part of any good relationship. If you aren't lonely to begin with you don't even want a relationship, and once you are in a relationship, what keeps you in it is the loneliness. I'm convinced that is why the couples who learn how to miss each other when they are apart, rather than feel damn glad to be free for a day, a night, or a weekend, are the ones who stay together.

One day I said to Ben, "Do you really think that life is about finding someone you never want to be without, and possibly couldn't even live without?" He said "Yes." That's when the trouble began.

Ben's saying yes made me angry even though he gave me the answer I was expecting to hear. I cleared my throat and said: "I've got this sort of now you see it now you don't philosophy on life. The main thing I know is that life is most definitely 'not' about anything. It's a biological process. Just because humans have the ability to analyze and assess every damn thing doesn't mean that there is any payoff once you do. We don't try to evaluate the meaning of a hippopotamus's or a daffodil's life and they go through much the same processes we humans do. I don't understand why life has to be *about* anything, I'd be content just learning how to get from point A to point B." Ben said my lack of enthusiasm and romance was disparaging of him and he couldn't understand how I lived at all with such a pessimistic outlook. I told him that was because things just seemed to happen to me. Then, for some reason, I told him I couldn't live with him anymore.

The day I moved out of Ben's I took the crock-pot and my bag of yo-yos. Ben was livid. He demanded that I leave behind my pink butterfly yo-yo; it was the one that had entangled us. I complied. He told me yo-yos were a wicked fascination and not safe for a person of my temperament. I told him that he ought to leave the crayons in the bathroom. I took a solid breath, sucking in the scent of that apartment, storing it away in my olfactory cupboard, and then I walked out the door, just before Ben put his fist through it.

IV.

After I left Ben, I wandered around for a while. By traveling the sidewalk express, I met some of those folks with the signs. They were some of the most fascinating people I'd ever met. One of the old men I got to know had once been a stock-broker on Wall Street. That's what he said. He said that life these days is artificial and all about "things." He said that leaving things had made him whole. I offered him a yo-yo as a token of our friendship. He declined; he didn't want anything, he said.

I got an apartment just before winter hit. It was warm—utilities included, I think—and it smelled good and salty. My shape began to change in the six months after I left Ben. I no longer felt his sticky arms around me or his wet breath on my skin and it felt good. I felt whole. I wouldn't say that I sprung back, but Ben's indentations were no longer noticeable.

The new apartment had a personality all its own. It shone like ocean water on a seashell in the sun. Its scent was like the sea too, and it was bathed in yellows. There was no shower curtain. I took baths. I was living with Jim at the time. He never took baths; he took showers. He liked the way the tile floor in the bathroom felt when it was glistening with water. We used to play on it like children in a six-inch-deep swimming pool—half naked and sliding. I never slept with him, though.

Jim was one of the men I met on the sidewalks. He also believed that there were too many "things" these days; only unlike me and most of the people I'd met, he had a job.

Jim was a walking salesman, door-to-door I guess it's called. He would have worked for the Fuller Brush Company if it had been the Fifties but it wasn't. So he sold shower curtains and other bathroom stuff for a company in Springerville.

He liked my yo-yos, wanted to sell them. We used to sit and talk about things all the time. He wasn't concerned with getting from point A to point B but he did travel a straight line. We talked about yo-yo factories and yo-yos the size of truck tires. I never bought into it—his idea of becoming the greatest yo-yo manufacturer ever by just selling the most. He was fascinated with his own stories, though, and I liked to encourage him. He could be a lot of fun when we were talking about yo-yos.

I lived with Jim just long enough—got my fill—then I left. What I liked most about him was that I didn't have to mold at all to live with him. Jim let me breathe. He didn't *take* my air. He didn't make me do anything. *He* didn't do much of anything. We didn't do much of anything together.

I made sure I took my yo-yos when I left. Jim offered me quite a few things he didn't have, trying to get me to leave the yo-yos behind. But I didn't. I wouldn't sell them; I wouldn't let anybody else sell them either.

It was spring again. The yo-yos danced and jumped and rolled in the sunlight—free again. I was homeless again. I had my bag of yo-yos and I had talked Jim out of a shower curtain. It was then I realized I had truly broken away from Ben. I no longer needed anything *he* had. I was free, I thought—until I met Rob.

V.

Rob taught me that I wasn't free. He also taught me that I ought to travel light. He hated my yo-yos; he wanted to get rid of them. He didn't want to sell them, though; he wanted to hurl them from a building.

Three weeks of Rob was all I could take and even that was too much. We didn't even live together. He had his block on the sidewalk express and I had mine. That was close enough.

It was around this time, the spring after Jim and the summer of actually fearing Rob, that I really began to assess all the thoughts I'd been having since before I met Ben—since after my father did it—and I last thought about doing it, about killing myself. I thought about cohabitation, about point A and point B, about relationships between the sexes, about men, about women, about pomegranates. That is when I was certain I would never think about doing it again.

VI.

Relationships between the sexes are like pomegranates—fleshy, sweet, and full of seeds. The trick to eating a pomegranate is: hold it in the palms of your hands, suck all the juice you can from its flesh, and spit out the seeds. Never swallow the seeds. The flesh stains your hands and your face. Swallowing the seeds seems to stain everything; it's as if the crimson dye seeps in and never fades. This stain, not so much an indentation, but a marking of sorts, is permanent.

Getting from point A to point B does not have to leave you stained like it did my dad. Point A to point B—it's a lot like traveling the sidewalk express. You are never really going anywhere, just traveling, just being. Along the way you meet people—sometimes incredible people—and you collect them, and you collect things. These you drag around with you in a bag. I collected men and yo-yos. I had a bag full of both, until recently.

VII.

I don't know why men and women cohabitate. I used to wonder about it. I don't anymore.

Last night a woman spent the night with me at my apartment. She was very beautiful. She was soft and fleshy and sweet.

I no longer collect yo-yos. I'm not a collector of anything now. I no longer need to drag things around in a bag or hide delicate things in glass jars.

I rolled the yo-yos I had, one by one, off a bridge and into a river. Except one. One small, purple butterfly yo-yo. It hasn't even got a string.

He Undertook Her

"Have you ever seen *Six Feet Under*?"

He was filling out the form for my father's cremation. He had just finished asking me for my dad's place of birth. My father died yesterday, in a car accident. He was living at a retirement home and had made dinner plans. He shouldn't have been driving. He was eighty-three, near-sighted, and his reflexes weren't very good. But he didn't have anything to bring to a dinner, so he ventured out to the CVS at the last minute, and turned left in front of a Chevy pick-up.

He looked up, "Yeah, a few times."

"I know it probably sounds funny, my asking you that, but I was just wondering, y'know. It's a pretty interesting show to me, since I'm not in the funeral business."

What I was really thinking is, the people on the show seem like regular people, they seem normal, well, sort of. I mean, they have typical problems, even though they work around dead people all day. They are still falling in love and having sex and being elated and being depressed and all that.

"No, it's not really strange your asking me," he chuckled, nervously, never looking up, as he continued to fill out the form, his bicep flexing and straining under his navy blue suit jacket.

"Well, what do you think of it? Do you think the show is accurate? I'm asking because I'm a teacher and they never portray teachers accurately on TV. I mean, they are usually either over-the-top inspirational, or really demeaning, or just looking to seduce some poor unsuspecting student. Do you think that on *Six Feet Under* they are accurately portraying the funeral business or is it all Hollywood like everything else?"

"What was your father's date of birth?"

"February 24th, 1926," I said, fiddling with the hem on my shirt.

He wrote in the date.

I waited, noting the smile lines around his mouth and the five o'clock shadow breaking through his crisp cheeks.

"What was his profession?"

"Writer."

I continued to play with the hem on my shirt.

"So?"

"So, yeah, it's pretty interesting your asking me that." He sat back in his chair a bit, finally lifting his dark brown eyes from the paper. He glanced around the room, looking ceiling-ward, then back down at the shiny black shoe on his right foot which was crossed over his left pinstriped leg. He leaned even farther back, contemplating, then sort of shot forward out of his contemplation and picked up his pen.

"Yes, I'd say it's pretty accurate, at least the regular day-to-day stuff. They don't show a lot of what it's really like, day *after* day, because they seem to be focused on love lives and death and that sort of thing, but they do kind of show the day-to-day in and outs. I guess it's just not all that dramatic most times."

I stared down at my feet. It's not all that dramatic—for *him.* People die. That's what they do. He cleans up the mess. That's what he does. All six-feet-two, three, one of him.

"I mean, it's not dramatic like it is on TV. People aren't ummm…."

"Dying every day?" I asked, with an awkward smile and raised brows.

"Well, um, yes, they are, but…" and now his smile was awkward, his brows furrowed.

"It's okay, I know what you mean," I began, my voice trailing off a bit with each word, and then with a sudden burst of emotion, speaking at a higher pitch and with a sweeping finality: "I get it."

We finished filling out the paperwork. While he was crunching the numbers, I looked around at the walls. There were a lot of framed degrees and certificates. Not all of them were in his name. It's a family business, I realized. His dad or brother or uncles or something were on the walls with him. They were all Bentleys.

"So, is this what you always wanted to do, Adam Bentley? Or are you like a Jameson, you are born a Jameson, y'know—Jameson's Irish Whiskey—and you just know what you are going to do? I was in Dublin, and they had the family tree of John Jamesons at the distillery, and yeah, well, it was pretty clear what you were going to do if you were born a Jameson, *boy,* that is."

"Yeah, actually, it is. I grew up in this house, we lived upstairs when I was a kid. This was my home and it was nice always having my family around. It was, uh, homey. I guess that's sort of weird to other people, but to me it was home. My dad was always around and there were always people in our house, and I liked that."

"But wasn't it hard seeing people crying all the time?"

"Well, yes and no. I guess when I was really little my parents kept me away from that part of it, but when I got a bit older, I liked being able to be around. Being around kids always makes people act differently, so when I was around seven or eight, they just seemed to focus on me, and I guess, well, sort of pull it together."

"Oh," I said, remaining fairly pulled together.

"I'm sorry, I'm really sorry about your father."

"It's okay. I mean, it's not okay, but it's okay. He was older… not that that makes it okay, but…it's not like I didn't know it was coming," I said, looking sideways and clearing my throat. "He was going to die, it's just, well, you just never know when, I guess. I guess that's it, you just never know when."

The sun was streaming through the front window in a beam that lit up a framed picture that sat on his desk, slightly tilted in my direction, slightly tilted in his, of what I presume was his wife and daughters. His prominent and unabashed display of his family was a reminder that the last member of my family was lying somewhere in this building. I suddenly wanted to take the ideal family smiling at me so exuberantly from an ornate metal frame and stuff it into my purse.

"Are you ready to start talking about what you want to do with the remains? Since he is going to be cremated, we will have his ashes next week, and you will want to decide what you would like to do with them. Are you going to be burying them or scattering them?"

I stared at him blankly. I hadn't heard what he had asked; I was too busy trying to figure out how to steal his family and fit them in my bag. Well, not his family exactly, but at least that 5 x 7 framed picture.

"What?"

"Are you going to be burying them or scattering them?"

"Uh…um…I don't really know. Do I have to decide that now?"

"Well, no, not really, but if you'd like me to let you know what your options are…."

"Yes, I'd like to know the options," I said, suddenly self-assured. "I like having all the information I can to make a decision," I said firmly.

"Okay, well, then, I'll have to take you downstairs. That's where we have the various containers. There are some that are designed for burial, and some that are designed for keeping in the home. We also have keepsakes, if you plan on burying or scattering the ashes, but would also like a keepsake."

A keepsake? Like, I take a leg or a cheek and I put them in a jar? Or, I suppose once a person is melted down like that it's not really a leg or a cheek but more like a goulash of some kind. I stared at his cheek again. His smooth, fairly youthful, only slightly creased cheek.

"Downstairs is fine," I said, half-imagining the embalming room on *Six Feet Under* while realizing that was not where he was planning to take me.

"I really don't know what I want."

"That's okay. People often don't, but I'll show you, and that might help you decide."

We proceeded to the elevator. It was old. He pulled the metal door closed and then pushed the button. The elevator lurched into service, and down we went, into the crypt. For a moment I felt a panic attack coming on, as I continued to imagine an embalming room.

When we exited, there were caskets everywhere—an entire room of caskets sitting on plush beige carpeting enclosed by cream-colored walls. These were the shorter ones, probably five feet. Displaying the 6'8 ones like my father's would take up a lot of room, I supposed, and they wouldn't want to unnerve people with baby-sized ones.

Then we took a quick right, and we were in a room of vases, or so it seemed to me. Little green and blue ones and tall ones that were of solid pewter. And gold and floral ones.

"These smaller ones are the keepsakes I was mentioning. If you think you might bury or scatter, but would like a keepsake, these would be appropriate. What we would do is, when you came to pick up the remains, we would have the keepsake for you, sealed, and you could display it on a small stand. We would also have the rest of the remains in one of these burial boxes, or in a temporary case for scattering."

The remains of what? What is this container going to contain, exactly?

"We make sure that the keepsake is sealed, so that there is no possibility of…."

Escape, I thought, "I see," I said. "I suppose one of these keepsakes would be just fine. What are my options with the burying and scattering thing again?"

"These containers are for burial," he said, gesturing, with the cloth again tight against his strong, secure upper arm, toward one wall, "and the ones for scattering we don't really display, because they are just temporary."

Temporary, like our lives, I thought. "I pick the blue one," I said. "He has amazing blue eyes. Well, he *had* amazing blue eyes"… which will now be in my keepsake, maybe … "so I'll pick that one."

We decided on the scattering box, because it's cheaper, and I could always get a burial box later.

As we exited the container room, I inquired, "So, which one of these caskets is the most expensive?"

His mahogany eyes lit up.

"Well, um, it depends. This one over here is the most expensive all around," he said excitedly, leading me to a pretty one towards the back. "It's made of copper, has 24 karat gold embellishments, a champagne velvet interior, a lock system, and an adjustable bed mattress," he said without taking a breath.

"Adjustable mattress?" I blurted out. "A lock system?" "Who's trying to get *in*?" I choked my words out as I doubled over with laughter. *Escape. Now.*

"Well, sometimes there are grave robbers, and also the adjustable bed," he started to say solemnly, almost retracting, trying to explain, and then a smirk broke and he started laughing too.

And there we were, both laughing, but I began laughing so hard that I began choking out tears, and that's when I reached for his sturdy arm to steady myself on my right, and a galvanized steel casket to steady myself on my left. There we were, sandwiched between caskets, me laughing hysterically one moment, me crying the next.

And he stepped right up, like he'd been doing it all his life, which I knew he had. He put an awkward tight arm around me and there we stood, with me sobbing into his navy blue pinstriped stoical lapel.

The Feet, mechanical, go round…this is the Hour of Lead… Remembered if outlived…. The Feet, mechanical, go round…this is the Hour of Lead….

After I composed myself, I demurely wiped my nose on my sleeve and walked numbly to the elevator, following his postured lead, both of us in silence.

When we arrived on the first floor, he asked if I was alright. I assured him I was. After a long pause, he then told me that the remains of my father would be back by Wednesday, Thursday at the latest. *His last trip*, I realized.

"We'll give you a call when they arrive," he said, and I winced at the use of the third person plural for my father, the writer.

"Thank you, Adam," I said, and walked briskly out the door.

Then I headed directly to Barnes and Noble to buy a copy of *Stiff: The Curious Lives of Cadavers*, which I had heard reviewed on NPR several years before. I wanted to know where my father was going next.

Rotary Dial

Chuck reached for the phone. He had never talked much on the phone and had never much liked it. He wasn't that sort of man. He had been the sort of man who awoke at 4:00 a.m., even on weekends, dressing fully before leaving his bedroom by pulling on his worn boots with certainty and buttoning his shirt carefully with his calloused hands. He would then pour a plastic Casey's General Store cup of black coffee, and be on the way to the farm in his Ford F-150 with the cup screwed into its base on the dash by 4:15. He was a man of many expressions but few words. His eyes, black holes deep in their sockets, and his mouth, set tightly against the backdrop, were pointed enough. A pursing of the lips and a slight squint and he said his piece while pacing a length.

But this morning Chuck reached for the phone. Ever since Ethel died, he made calls. He dialed randomly at first, willing to speak to anyone who answered the line. Sometimes he reached businesses and would engage in some sort of inquiry. What are your hours today? Is Lisa (a suitably common name) in today? I was wondering if I could make an appointment. Yes, two o'clock on Saturday is fine. I am wondering what it would cost to refinance my house. I am wondering if I could get a better deal on life insurance. Car insurance? What sorts of ve-hicles do you sell? Sorry, I must have the wrong number. Other times he would reach a residence. I must have misdialed. Are you sure Dave (another suitably common name) isn't there? But this is the number I have for my daughter, and it can't be wrong. Are you a friend of Archie's? He told me I should call you about a problem I'm having with my radiator.

Then Chuck started calling for Ethel. He asked every woman who answered the line if she was Ethel. (He hung up on the men.) He dialed outside his area code. No sense risking reaching someone he actually did know. Sometimes he would reach someone who would stay on the line 45 seconds or more. Other times the person would hang up without even saying that Chuck had reached the wrong number. Sometimes he was taken for a telemarketer. Once he was yelled at for calling during supper. Once he dialed a sex line.

Then one Saturday, before the coffee Chuck had poured had even cooled, he dialed Ursula.

"Hello? Is Ethel there?"

"Who?"

"Ethel, I'm calling for Ethel."

"No, Ethel isn't here, just me, Ursula."

"Oh, sorry, Ursula, I was just trying to reach Ethel."

"Oh, that's okay, Ursula, Ethel, what's the difference? They sort of sound the same, don't they?"

"Yes, I suppose they do. But, I don't know, what sort of a name is Ursula, anyway?"

"I think it's Latin. I don't know. We're German. Strong German stock. Ursula sounds German, doesn't it? It sounds more German than Latin. Who is Latin anymore? I mean, unless you're talking about Latinos, but that's not the same thing, is it?"

Chuck wondered if it was. He never knew anyone who was Latin or Latino, he didn't think. He knew Ethel, and she was English and Irish. She had curly grey hair she had kept close to the head, but long enough for him to pull on her curls with affection. When they were young, her hair had been auburn and long past her shoulders. She had worn it styled, often in a braid of some sort to manage those curls, which were not in fashion then, and Chuck would reach around to tug on them gently when he hugged her, or when she was doing the dishes and her back was to him, or she was occupied with some thing or another. When Ethel got older, she stopped trying to curb her hair or Chuck's affections, and she'd also kept Chuck closer and closer by her side. After they both knew Ethel was sick, Chuck hardly left the house. He hadn't been good at helping with her hair, then, and it became wilder than it had ever been, splayed out in different directions around her pillow, but Chuck didn't mind and Ethel let it go.

Chuck and Ursula talked while Ursula sipped her coffee in Arizona. Chuck lived in North Dakota. He had never been to Arizona. It didn't much matter to him where Ursula was, though. He was just happy to be talking to her. And then Ursula said she had to go. She was going to go do some garage sale hunting and "the early bird gets the worm." "It was nice talking to you, Chuck. I hope you find Ethel," she said and hung up.

Chuck missed Ethel even more now. But he didn't know what number he had dialed to reach Ursula and that made the absence even more profound. He had been told he should update his phone, but he didn't see anything wrong with a rotary dial. He didn't understand why everything had to be updated. Things were good as they were.

Chuck began dialing randomly, trying to reach Ursula again, but he kept getting the usual responses from the people who picked up. Now he would say, "Ethel?" And then, "Ursula?" And then when the woman said no to both, he would get an even greater sinking feeling.

And then Chuck's monthly phone bill came. When he pulled it from the envelope, he realized it had all the long distance numbers he had dialed all month, with the dates and times. It was easy to remember the day he had reached Ursula, and now he had her number. But now that he had it, he didn't know what he should do with it. Could he call her again? Should he? Was he being too presumptuous? He'd heard someone say that once, that certain things were presumptuous. He'd heard that at The Golden Biscuit. The waitresses were talking about how it was presumptuous to go out on a date with a man and expect him to pay for dinner. Chuck had never thought about that. He'd always paid for dinner when he and Ethel went out, even before they were married. Wasn't that what a man was supposed to do? He had also opened Ethel's car door, and helped her on with her coat, and pulled out her chair at The Golden Biscuit. All these things he was overhearing about new rules were confusing to him. Ethel had always thanked him for such things. The only time she swatted him away was when he tried to help her in the kitchen. She had always said that was her way of opening the door for him, or pulling out his chair. He just needed to "sit down and eat." He hadn't been eating much since Ethel died.

Chuck didn't know if he should call Ursula or not, but he couldn't help himself. He looked in the mirror as he dressed the morning he decided he would call again. His flannel wasn't curving out in the middle like it used to. His shoulders were now sloping and his belly was not.

"Ursula?"

"Yes?"

"Hi, it's Chuck."

"Oh, the man from North Dakota? Did you ever find Ethel?"

"Well, no, not exactly, but I did think that maybe we could talk a bit more, that is, if you aren't going out to the garage sales."

"Oh, no, Chuck, I don't go to garage sales on Wednesdays. Wednesdays I quilt. Let me pour a cup of coffee. Do you like coffee, Chuck? I just love coffee. I can drink a pot a day. The doctors say you shouldn't but I don't get that reasoning. People should worry more about all those things they stick in 2-liters… or their noses! Coffee never did anything to hurt anyone and I drink mine black. How do you take your coffee, Chuck? Why don't you pour yourself a cup and we can sit down together and chat? I could sure use the company."

Ursula began describing her quilt projects and stitches and the gals that belonged to the quilting club with her, and Chuck just listened. He listened more than he probably had ever listened because just the lilt of Ursula's voice soothed him.

Chuck began to imagine Ursula as he leaned his head back in his easy chair. He hoped Ursula didn't have curly hair or blue eyes. He hoped she was different. He didn't want her to be like Ethel. He wanted Ethel to stay just the way she was and Ursula to be Ursula. All that he imagined was Ursula kept pouring through the phone. The talk was all.

And that is what started it. A misdialed number, looking for Ethel, and Chuck had found Ursula. Now Chuck missed

Ethel a little bit less most days, and Ursula a little bit more others.

When Chuck was lonesome, he dialed Ursula. It made him feel good. And he began eating again. One day Ursula was going to cook "a ham steak and some fried potatoes," she said. When they hung up so Ursula could cook dinner, Chuck ordered from The Golden Biscuit, raced to pick it up, and called Ursula back. He said he hoped he wasn't interrupting, but he'd like to talk over dinner, and so they did. They listened to each other chew and take drinks and in between the talking and chewing, there was laughter.

One Monday afternoon, the phone startled Chuck when it rang.

"Chuck? It's Ursula. I hope you don't mind me calling. It feels…so…forward of me, I was just, I was just pouring myself a cup of coffee and I…."

"Ursula?"

"Yes?"

"Thank you…for calling."

The Grief Eater

You,

who cannot tell your grief,

join me.

I can consume

nations of sufferers

entire.

I am the good parasite –

huge,

limbless,

noisome,

beautiful.

Let me live.

– Frank Fagan, "The Good Parasite"

I wore my black dress. It was sunny. The long sleeved one. It was 84 degrees. I didn't eat anything. It was a size too small. My hand steady but heart pounding, I signed the guest book Maria, and then I went to the ladies' room. I looked ghastly. My skin was pale, too pale against my straightened black hair, my eyes were dark, grim. My lips were too red. It was my first time. I took a deep breath and cupped my hands beneath the water and drank. I dabbed my mouth with a paper towel. I inhaled deeply and walked calmly out the bathroom door.

I read it in the paper, the news about the 87-year-old man who went to bed quite literally with a bump on his head and never awoke again. He was going to be at the funeral home on 48th and there would be a memorial service on Sunday, September 2nd.

Once inside Room C, I discovered there were too few seats. One in the center of the second row left, one on the left in the sixth row right. There were fifteen rows, twenty across, nearly full; he was not alone.

I made my way to the sixth row right. I sat next to an old woman with bluish hair that matched her blue dress. She had an embroidered handkerchief in her hand, and a black purse with a large metal buckle on her lap that looked like a doctor's bag. She made an effort to smile. Our arms brushed as I sat down. "Excuse me," I said, and she crunched up her mouth in an effort to be kind without words. I sucked on a mint.

The ceremony was also kind. He'd lived a good life. He'd been a son first, then a sibling, a soldier, a husband, father, grandfather, great grandfather. It was not an extraordinary life, but it was probably mostly good, or at least he was. He'd probably had watermelon on hot Sundays in summer. I'm sure he didn't hug much, but when he did, it was fierce. I'm sure he drank occasionally. I'm sure he was a good worker, less so a lover, but that he'd been better with his great grandchildren than with any children that came before. I am also certain that when he died his hands were still calloused.

When it ended, I excused myself again and slipped out the main door. Then I bought a watermelon and ate the whole thing.

Monday afternoon I went to the funeral home on 64th. This time it was for a child, a little boy. He'd accidentally hanged himself on a swing set his parents had just built. His sister had seen it happen. She was six. She was not at the service.

I wore a baby blue dress. Black did not seem fitting for a child.

He was beautiful. He had bright red hair and freckles. He still had baby fat. He wasn't dressed in a suit. He wore a sailor's hat, a pair of navy blue swimming trunks, and a hooded green sweatshirt. He was going to the beach. He'd lived in Iowa his entire short life; he'd never been to the beach.

There was talk about his favorite toys: a fire engine, a dog with a missing eye named Fred. They were in his casket. His mother sat still, barely breathing. The father, he was mannered. He smiled. He nodded. He stood motionless. The preacher spoke of angels, of love, of sandboxes, of summer. He tried to make sense out of none. He knew the boy. The boy had had grandparents on both sides and a great grandmother on one. It wasn't right.

I spoke with the great grandmother. She remembered me. She knew me from church, or the church picnic, or at least she thought she did. She thanked me for coming; she thanked me for my blue dress. She said that all the black in the room made it seem like it was a funeral when it was just a day at the beach. Then she walked away, chewing gum.

This morning I clipped the obituaries from the paper, carefully curving the scissors, exactingly isolating the names. I organized the type on the table, from young to old, then the women and girls, men and boys. Then I organized them according to the number of people who had survived them. Then I organized them according to which ones had a photograph and which didn't; then which funeral home; then alphabetically by name. I settled on alphabetically by name. It was the only way that seemed, ultimately, fair.

The album I had purchased at the store was an acid-free, three-ring binder. I could add more pages if I wanted, whenever necessary. I spent most of the morning carefully placing the obituaries in order from Brimer to Thompson. I occasionally reconsidered my choice of assemblage.

I would see the Croftons on Thursday. Mr. and Mrs.— newlyweds. Car crash. Alcohol involved, but they weren't drinking. I wore a dark blue pantsuit and a red wig. I was back on 48th; the funeral director looked at me quizzically, with confused, or maybe concerned, recognition. The Croftons had no children, but they had parents: two on one side and a father on the other. I embraced the father, Joe, and explained I was a co-worker of Mrs. Crofton, his daughter. I knew what she did and where she worked—the paper had told me. She was beautiful, I said. She was always punctual, pleasant, and perceptive. There were times when she had comforted me. I was momentarily his daughter incarnate and I glowed, if not for him, then for me. He longed for her and for now I had given a part of her back to him. I also gave him a mint.

November was a cold month. Winter came quickly—autumn had left us in early October. I drank a lot of coffee and had too many dreams. I wore leg warmers in the living room, but sweatpants to bed. The obituaries were abundant. The cold had caught some by surprise, particularly the poor. Furnaces needed repair; electric bills had gone up.

Pneumonia was rampant. I had walking pneumonia and I didn't want to get anyone sick. I found myself busy with my album. Of particular interest was the single man, 38, who worked out of his home. He'd fallen asleep at his computer. His neighbor had left a cigarette burning when she went out dancing. Three apartments had burned, but he was the only one home on a Saturday night. The funeral was the following Saturday evening at six. I made a beautiful widow. My black dress was cut above the knee and nearly below the breast. I was on a date, though no one else knew it.

Hair curled, cheeks pinched, I sauntered in this time. I wanted to give him what should have kept him home on a Saturday, not literally, but figuratively. There was a small turnout, mostly what seemed to be other stay-at-home boys in their thirties and forties. I raised eyebrows. Bill spoke to me, as did Tom, and Rick. How did I know the deceased? Was he a freelancer for my company? Was I one of the other neighbors? Was I family? I explained that I lived in an apartment building down the block, and that we had bumped into each other frequently since we seemed to keep similar schedules. Tom offered that I must have been talking about his early morning visit to the Grind & Brew. I agreed. There was much smiling. Too bad I didn't know him better they said. I again agreed.

They were desperate for me, not only in their grief but with their sex. They were lonely, all three of them, lonely for a life that would not end like my not-so-handsome, but horribly appealing man-boy, lying in wait for me in his casket. I hugged them each. I cried. No, I sobbed. Then I reapplied my lipstick in the ladies' room, fluffed my hair, rejoined them momentarily, giggled appealingly, and walked out one foot directly in front of the other as I'd once been taught models do to make their hips swing all the more seductively.

When I arrived home I wore a black negligee and created my altar. Little Boy Blue would rest on top of the short plastic table under the window in a light brown frame. I suppose it might seem strange to others, should they ever find him there, that his picture is a clipping from the paper. One would think I would have a real photograph of my lover. I spent some time dreaming about who he was to me. None of my scenarios seemed to work, except that perhaps I was his secret admirer. I'd desired him from afar in the coffee shop each morning and he died before I had a chance to reveal myself. It made the most sense, perhaps, because to at least some degree it was true, though I'd never before been in the Grind & Brew that I now frequented, especially on Saturdays when they made blueberry scones, my favorite, and I'd never met him alive. I did bring him espresso and a scone every Saturday now, though.

Winter was long. It seemed spring would never come. Boating accidents were far from a reality. There would be no swing set deaths in January, not February either. There were no roofers taking a plunge, no prom night car accidents. There were car accidents but not of the festive kind, not past New Year's anyway. Winter was for the lonely and the old, mostly, except for the skiing accidents, the snowmobiling, the black ice. I mostly kept inside when I wasn't at work. I mostly kept busy with my album.

I read my album and re-read it. I continued to debate my choice of assemblage. I could not make sense of the obituaries. They had an order, but there was no order to what they contained.

On a Wednesday the sun shone. I was emerging from a long hibernation. It had been raining for five days. Spring showers. Saturated earth. The rain had made it hard to bury the dead, and the roads were slick. There were numerous car accidents in the paper, more it seemed than there had been all winter. I went to my first funeral in months. It was that Thursday night. It was for another middle-aged man.

Although after the Croftons I no longer approached the same funeral home more than twice, if I could control myself, this time I saw someone who had been at the same funeral where I had been months before. I had been a co-worker before; I was a co-worker now. These were two different companies. The man was perplexed and a bit disturbed. He remembered me. Didn't I work for a computer company? Didn't I work with Joe? I had to explain I had only been working with Joe for a few months; I had previously worked with Sam. But I blush, so I blushed deeply. I thought I had been discovered. What to say? Who goes to funerals for people they don't know? You would think people would consider it nice, but they wouldn't. Why shouldn't we honor the dead though? Why aren't we allowed to honor the dead we don't know? What is so sick about it? I wanted to know.

I managed, awkwardly. I should have worn the red wig, I thought to myself. It makes me look unlike myself, I think. It also makes my blushing less apparent.

I left shaken, frightened, I had seen someone else's ghost. I stopped by the coffee shop. I ordered a latte. I held it between my hands remembering the cold, warming my hands with the heat of a latte on a 75-degree day. I was cold and more lonesome than I had yet been among my dead. I wanted the embrace of a warm body, the steaming of something more than a coffee cup.

When I returned home, I sat with Little Boy Blue and listened to the Beatles and rocked and cried, cried and rocked.. Little Boy Blue put me in a trance. We were alone but we were alone together. And then I wanted another funeral but I was afraid. Would they see inside? How could I reenter the world of the living among the dead?

I slept a long sleep. When I awoke, I sat at the kitchen table staring blankly at the obituaries in the newspapers that had been piling up on my doorstep. Where were they? Where were the ones I needed to find? I blinked, straining to read through tears. Where would I find them?

It was a family of four: father (38), mother (36), daughter (11), son (8), daughter (18 months). Murdered. I didn't know what to wear. I didn't know who I might be. How could I blend in? Who was she? He? The paper didn't say. Would anyone recognize me? Who might know me? My city seemed to be shrinking the more funerals I attended.

It was a grand outpouring. The entire city's population appeared to be there. The paper later reported that it was the largest funeral attended since the Mayor's. I felt utterly alone and inconsolable. There were so many people between them— the mother, the father, the children—and me. It was dizzying. I could barely breathe; the crowd was stifling. It was suffocating. When I rose to leave, every bump of the eyes left a gash. I made my jagged way. I was racked. I was keeling. I was going to give but I had nothing to offer. I despaired of purpose, and then numbly walked home.

I needed to embrace and be embraced by the grieving; I needed to console the inconsolable, so my next appearance was at a baby's funeral. I thought no one would wonder why I was there. Certainly no one would suspect I knew the baby. I couldn't be a co-worker; I could just blend into the crowd; there would certainly be a crowd.

Sally had died in her crib. The article in the paper was educational, intended to inform current and future parents of the threat of Sudden Infant Death Syndrome. The church community was reaching out to the family, would hold a benefit, donations could be given to a local organization dedicated to the support of bereaved families of SIDS.

I wore the baby blue dress again. I could hear my footsteps as I walked into the church. My steps reverberated from the ornate ceilings. I thought perhaps that I was in the wrong church. Perhaps it was the church down the street? As I entered the cathedral, I saw only two rows of mourners, the priest, and the casket. The casket was very small and white. It was closed. It looked like a toy, like a doll's crib, only enclosed. My heels clicked and heads turned. The sudden onslaught froze me. It was quickly clear that this was a private funeral, family only. They stared at me and I at them. One, two, three, four, the seconds passed as I stood frozen in place. I quickly considered my next course of action, to speak or not to speak, how to undo what I had done, how to minimize my intrusion. I nodded with understanding and turned and slowly walked towards the door, aware of the eyes penetrating the back of my dress. I considered the possibilities. They certainly couldn't be thinking that I had intended to arrive at the baby's funeral. No, I must have gotten the church wrong. I was supposed to be somewhere else. I wasn't wearing black; perhaps I was on my way to a wedding and it was simply a mix-up. Perhaps I thought there was a mass this afternoon. Maybe I was coming to confession? Did I have something to confess?

I sat in my car, staring emptily forward. I had heard only the key in the door, the closing of the latch, the sound of my positioning in the seat. What was I doing? I didn't know but I couldn't stop. I needed to do this; it needed to be done. Not for me, no not for me, this isn't about me, I insisted, but about them, for them—the others—the ones who need me.

I gathered myself. Then, on a beautifully sunny day, I wore a white linen skirt and an ivory blouse and I attended the funeral of a woman close to my age who had had an aneurysm. There was no warning. She was standing next to the water cooler at work filing papers into a cabinet when she fell. I didn't know this until I arrived at the funeral home, of course. She had been surrounded by people but she had been alone. She had lived alone, like me. She was single, like me.

The funeral attendees were mostly co-workers. She had a brother. He was unable to be thankful, unable to speak. He sat alone in the front row wringing his hands, head down. I sat alone in the third row left, an unoccupied void between us, watching him wring his hands and wondering how I would stand and leave, how my legs would support me, whether I could walk without collapsing.

I suddenly realized that I had been and was an uninvited *guest.* I looked at the brother again, eyes darting from him to the *outsiders*—the co-workers—and to him again and again, and again, rapidly. And then I turned my eyes on myself: I am *not family.* I am *not a friend.* I am *not a co-worker.* I am *nobody.* I am *not here.* I cannot be *here.*

The room was dizzying as I clung to the chair, my mouth suddenly dry and full. It was as though I had been eating all afternoon. I could eat no more. I clasped my hands fearfully over my lips. It was like trying to trap hundreds of escaping flies inside a jar. The purging, the swirling abundance, I thought I would vomit and then lurch forward onto the floor.

My mind darted from idea to idea, spinning, spiraling. But this could not be about me, this woman's funeral; it must be about her. I had no right to steal this moment from her, this brief moment. I had no right to take it from her brother, to try and absorb his pain.

And then I saw it.

I was there on the altar. I was in white, I was white, and the room was empty. There were no black suits, no blue dresses, no ivory blouses. I saw myself rifling the pages of my album, my guestbook. My guestbook was blank, except for my name on the first page, the pages of my album now nothing but acid-free blankness—the terror. Sheer whiteness sandwiched between endless carnival-mirrored black leather uniformity, and then all went blue.

They were framed perfectly: my sister (hit and run, 12), mother (breast cancer, 39), father (heart attack, 52), brother (suicide, 27), and Little Boy Blue were standing behind him and beside him, smiling.

There above me, not wringing his hands, not waiting for me, but peering down was the dead woman's brother, digesting it all, eating my grief, like thousands of flies feasting. And then I felt an embrace.

Dressing the Part

The dress was boxed in 1990. The box still had the dry cleaner's receipt attached to its slightly yellowed side. Behind the cellophane window, Eva could just glimpse the beaded back of the dress; its accompanying veil kept the dress partly veiled. The veil itself had ivory flowers decorated with pearls adorning the headband and trailing tulle sprinkled with more pearls and edged with ribbon. Eva recalled its cascade down her back. Her auburn hair had at the time been shoulder-length, though she had worn it twisted up into ribbons and bound with matching pearl-adorned ivory flowers. While her hair had been up, she remembered fondly how the cascade of the veil had felt like she had had hair reaching to the small of her back. As she danced in the arms of Nick so many years ago, swaying back and forth, back and forth, it had swung and swung, lightly teasing her back, largely bare, due to the plunging lines of the dress. Eva leaned her back against the headboard and closed her eyes. Swinging her head quietly and intently from side to side, she imagined the veil's delicate touch glancing off her back once more.

Eva's hair was now a short bob of grey. The slate green of her eyes just as bright, if only the white around them hadn't become a bit more yellowed and blood shot with age. Eva stroked the outside of the similarly aged box she had hauled out of the closet while sorting some of Nick's things. Several black trash bags were lumps on the floor beside the bed. Eva sat up, leaned over a bit, and peered through the window, considering whether she should upset the archival sanctity of the gown. She heard the creak of the king-sized bed as she leaned. Their marriage bed. Eva slid down on her back and looked up.

She and Nick had shared this bed so many nights. Sometimes they slept curled toward, sometimes away from each other. Sometimes they would lie on their backs staring up at the speckled ceiling chatting away into the night about work, the children, their future, then collapse into giggling fits as something funny occurred to them or their signature word play was introduced. Other nights they read in bed side by side, occasionally pausing to read a passage to one another or ask a question about some word, place, or idea evoked. As Eva looked up now, she noticed how the lace curtains draped over the canopy, and despite their constant presence, she took the lace curtains as a sudden indication of what she must do.

Eva's waist had broadened with each child. They had had three, two years apart. The third was still at home, the second had just left, and the first had been away two years at college. Eva remembered a woman of about her current age, 56, commenting on Eva's own "lovely waist" on her wedding night—Eva had nearly rushed the woman and her friend as she had entered the bed and breakfast with Nick. The woman had turned to her female companion and exclaimed, "Look at that lovely waist! I remember having a waist like that!" Eva hadn't at the time realized the full import of the comment. She now knew that woman had clearly known what she was talking about. Waists are not something that improve with age. "With each child the waist expands," Eva thought disappointedly, "at least two inches."

The dress was a size eight. She was now a size eight again, but she couldn't imagine her waist at all resembled the waist she had once had. Even after losing thirty pounds in the last six months, her waist had hardly budged, or so it seemed. "Budged or pudged?" It had pudged gradually over her marriage to Nick.

Eva stood abruptly and walked to the full-length mirror. She turned sideways. Her stomach was practically concave. She turned toward the front. She had always had something of an hourglass figure, but with a widened waist, she now appeared to be more boy shaped. More up and down. There was hardly a distinction between waist and hip. She'd stopped eating meals, snacking instead when she became so weak she had to have food, and she'd lost some of her hips, but less of her belly. She stood staring at herself. She lifted her shirt over her head. She stood in her bra. She removed her sweat pants and stood in her underwear and bra. She brushed some grey hair behind her right ear. She tilted her head to the side. Then she turned and leapt onto the bed with a sudden feeling of hope.

She flipped the box over. Of course it was taped shut. She lay on her belly across the bed and opened the end table drawer. There had to be something in there...a pen. That would do. She ran the pen through the tape on the four sides of the rectangular box and then quickly flipped the box back over. She took a deep breath. She closed her eyes for a moment. She opened them. She paused again. And then Eva began shaking the top of that box. After about five shakes, the bottom fell to the bed. There was the veil and the dress, arranged so perfectly the way the past still appeared vividly in her mind. Untouched.

Archived. She leaned over and breathed deeply. The dress didn't smell like Nick. It didn't smell like the fall day they had wed. It didn't smell like anything, except maybe an old piece of dry cleaning. First her heart sunk, but then her glee returned, "Nothing more to preserve then!" Eva hollered.

Eva reached in and grabbed the dress forcefully by its puffy shoulders. Crunch. They had filled those capped sleeves with tissue paper to make it hold the shape of her young shoulders. It was as though she had been folded and put into a box, stuffed and on display behind a cellophane window, only at the back of a darkened closet.

Eva quickly pulled the full length of the dress out of the box, jumped off the bed, and took two quick steps toward the mirror. She held the dress in front of her. The dress was so much younger than she was. It was so perfect. Fresh. Not yellowed like the box or her eyes. As she considered putting the dress back in the box, she stared at her reflection in the mirror, still holding it before her underweared nudity. She then went and sat on the bed, held the dress to her breast, and began sobbing. She had been thinking about the dress for days before she had gathered the energy to shove past what remained of Nick's things and remove it from the back of the closet.

Moments later, Eva stood and unzipped the dress. It was so soft. Stepping into it, she felt the satin fabric against her thighs and her sex momentarily awakened. It had been nearly dormant. Before sliding the dress up and over her shoulders, she unsnapped her bra and her 56-year-old breasts dropped from it. "They aren't 30 year-old breasts," she said to herself. She raised her arms above her head as she kept the dress from sliding down her now nearly absent hips by cocking her left leg up. Her breasts rose ever so slightly with the raising of her arms. "There, that's closer," she chuckled at her reflection as she contemplated whether plastic surgeons asked women to raise their arms above their heads to get an idea of where their breasts *once* were. She repeatedly lifted her arms over her head to test her theory, giggling aloud.

As Eva lifted the dress up and on to her forearms and then flabbier upper arms, she worried the dress wouldn't zip. The capped sleeves slid up and over. She turned her back to the mirror and began zipping. The zipper made it part way up, perhaps farther than she had expected, though it took some effort bending her arm to reach, but it was never going to make it past the breasts that had become fuller with children, too. That beautiful scoop back. It was going to have to be covered. With a sudden impish grin she recalled the ivory wool cape. She hadn't had to wear it that October day after all. It was still on its original hanger in a zipper bag in the downstairs closet.

Nearly tripping over the dress, then hoisting a handful with each fist, Eva practically hopped down the stairs to the hall closet and eagerly unzipped the garment bag. All she had to do was fasten the hook and eye at the throat and the cape would cover her bare age-spotted back but leave the wedding dress visible. She tore the cape off the hanger and tossed it over her shoulders. A quick hooking of the clasp and voila! Eva felt reborn, well almost.

Still standing inside the closet, Eva recalled how she had so adored that veil trailing down her back. She closed her eyes for just a moment to picture it and leaned her head on the wall. The dress suddenly felt heavier.

Pulling on the light string and closing the closet door, Eva thought about how few brides veiled their faces. Eva hadn't on her own wedding day, even though it was still the trend then. She wondered what mysterious quality was lost by being able to see the bride as she approached; she wanted to be mysterious.

Eva's cape was beginning to feel warm as she hobbled up the stairs clumsily to look at the veil. The dress wasn't sleeved, but it was many layered, and that cape was wool. She caught a glimpse of her flushed reflection in her bedroom mirror. She twirled. Smiled. Then grimaced. There were so many lines on her face. She didn't look at all like she once had. As she approached the mirror for further inspection, she noticed her chest was turning red. It was becoming splotchy, as was her face, from the heat. It was hot in here. After another awkward descent, she turned the thermostat to 60 degrees before climbing the stairs once again to consider the veil, huffing a bit as she continued to gather fists of gown in her hands, tiring with yet another sixteen steps to the second floor. She muttered under her breath, "Cinderella. Hrmph!"

The veil was so delicate. The comb only plastic and Eva wondered how it could secure itself enough in the grey hair she now had. Her hair was smoother, perhaps, or thinner than it had been. Pinching the comb of the veil between her thumb and forefinger she made it dance back and forth. While her grey bob typically was parted slightly to the left, she swung her head forward then shook her head back to stare at the ceiling again while she smoothed the crown of her head with her left hand, and then gently placed the veil in a gathering of hair with her right before re-positioning her head and gazing forward.

Eva practiced gliding around the room. She paused to look out the window, stopped and stared at some of the spines of the books on her shelf, then walked over to some of the portraits of the kids when they were babies. With the cape on she would be plenty warm if she went outside. She could hear the air blowing through the vents, but since she was on the second floor, she was still so hot, so she decided to return to the first and stand by the drafty front door.

While standing by the front door, she started to feel much more comfortable with the dress, with everything, so she opened the front door and walked out a few steps to stand by the porch railing.

The sun was starting to set and Julia would be home any minute from her part-time job at the mall. For just a moment while a car passed, Eva was self-consicous. She began to imagine Julia pulling into the drive while she was on the porch, but then she realized Julia, her girly-girl Julia, would love to see her mother in the dress. She would be so excited to see it out of the box that she might even want to try it on herself. Julia was slim, a perfect size six, with a perfect sixteen-year-old waist. Julia was also a romantic. She loved romantic comedies and *Seventeen* magazine and lip gloss, despite her mother's desires to turn her more towards dramas and Flannery O'Connor and Chapstick.

Eva went inside and walked carefully into the kitchen, managing not to snag the dress on any of the furniture. She was in the kitchen carefully eating a banana under her veil when Julia came in. "Mom! What are you doing? Oh my God, is that your dress from when you married Dad?" was followed by "Jeezus, it's cold in here. What do you have the air conditioning on?" Julia made her way to the thermostat before Eva could stop chewing the big chunk of banana she had shoved in her mouth. Eva lifted her dress and stretched her big toe far enough out from under it to hit the foot lever on the trash and toss her peel, and then she briskly walked after Julia. "Sixty degrees, Mom? What the heck?" "I was hot," Eva said dismissively as she made a sideways glance and shrugged her capped shoulders. Julia mumbled something about hot flashes and turned the thermostat up to 70, then whipped around quickly to focus on her mother again. "So, let me look at you! Mom, you look gorgeous! What made you take the dress out? It's so cool!" Julia fingered the tulle on the skirt, then reached for her mother's slim hips and made her do a full turn. "I always wanted you to get this dress out and let me see it. What's with the cape, though?" "I was cold," Eva said.

Suddenly past the excitement of the dress, Julia began walking back towards the kitchen talking to her mother while Eva stared after her daughter's perfect back. "So anyways, at work there was this annoying girl who wanted to try on, like, everything in the store," Julia began. Eva followed after her. Julia opened the fridge and looked inside. "She just kept ordering me around to get her different sizes and colors of everything as she shoved things over the top of the dressing room door," Julia said as she shut the fridge in favor of an apple on the counter. "I swear, Mom, what really sucked is the girl is in my homeroom. I hated having to wait on her like that," she said before she took a bite.

Eva offered some advice, "Yeah, that sucks, but those girls are always the ones whose aspirations are limited to dressing rooms," but Julia failed to see the humor and rolled her eyes as usual. "See ya later Mom," she said heading up to her room. Eva was left contemplating her limited capacity to connect.

As Eva sat at the kitchen table head down, feeling like a flop, she thought, "speaking of flop," as she stared at her breasts. They were very visible to her, if only because she had a direct view of her own cleavage. She decided to retreat back to her bedroom, this time with a twist-off bottle of white wine.

Eva stared at herself in the mirror and unscrewed the top of the bottle. She lifted the veil and took a swig.

She could most certainly wear it. She could save time getting ready from now on. Didn't Einstein do that? Wasn't he the one with all the same shirts and pants so he wouldn't have to think about clothes anymore? She wouldn't be too cold outside if she wore the cape, and no place was running their heat enough inside. Now that her circulation was poorer, she was often cold, anyway. She took another long swig and decided she could even wear the dress to bed.

Her quilt wasn't very thick, and with no warm body to keep her company, the bed had been feeling colder and colder. Nick had always generated so much heat.

After polishing off half of the bottle of wine while sitting on the edge of her bed in her dress, Eva got the munchies and went downstairs and popped some microwave popcorn. She finally settled into bed, removed the veil, and kicked her feet up with the bowl of popcorn and the rest of the wine. Julia texted away to her boyfriend in her next door bedroom as she often did at night. After taking so many flights of stairs, Eva knew she would be fine.

Eva awoke the next morning as if in a haze. She squinted and looked around the room. It was still very dark. The blinds were still closed and the sun wasn't quite up. At first she forgot she had gone to sleep in the dress and thought the bunch on top of her was the quilt wrapped around and around. When she lifted the quilt and couldn't see her toes because of the pouf of the dress, she was reminded what it was like to be pregnant. She was reminded of those babies on her ribcage, what it was like to lie on her back in the late months of pregnancy. Impossible. Sitting up in the dress now was a bit like that. Impossible. It took more effort to lift herself off of the bed and swivel her legs to the side than she had expected. The night came back to her as her head throbbed and she rubbed her eyes. "Maybe it was too much popcorn," she playfully said aloud, feeling like the crunchy leftover kernels she loved had popped, ballooning her stomach like an air popper fills a bowl.

Eva had some difficulty getting into the mini-van. The dress was even bigger than she had realized in the house. With the length and billow of the cape and the dress, and her eyes straining behind her progressive lenses from under the veil, getting into the van became an ordeal. She had tried moving her body in a familiar manner to get behind the steering wheel, but she got caught on the door and the wheel and couldn't wedge herself in. She tried pulling the dress tightly and coming in tautly to the side, the way she was used to squeezing out of the door when some idiot parked too close to the van, but that wasn't enough either. Huffing and puffing in the 40 degree weather, and coming at the seatback by leaning in from the backseat, she finally put the back as low as it would go and went around to the driver's seat and shoved herself and the dress in. The dress was about ten inches above her lap and held her elbows raised for her. She was going to drive with the tips of her fingers at ten and two. She was leaning far enough back that she was going to have to look left through a combination of the driver's side window and the backseat's side window. She looked in the rearview and then turned to look backwards as she backed out, but her veil caught and kept her head from turning completely. "Brides should not travel by minivan," she thought. "No wonder they take limos and horse-drawn carriages."

Barely reaching the pedals, Eva caught a glimpse of Julia out of the corner of her eye, who was now standing on the deck with her mouth agape, a cereal bowl in one hand, a spoon in the other. Eva gave her a queen's wave and gunned it out of the driveway.

This was Wednesday.

By the end of the weekend, Eva was getting into the driver's seat with greater ease, at least partly due to the wear and tear on the dress. By then, she also realized she had been doing it all partly wrong.

Sunday night she tapped small holes into the bottoms of several soup and fruit cans with a screwdriver and a hammer while Julia was at work. She lined the cans carefully with wax paper and then filled them each to the brim before covering them with aluminum foil and a rubber band.

Eva attached the soup cans to the trailer hitch of the mini-van with a rope in the early morning hours on Monday, while Julia still slept. She didn't give the cape or gown a thought as she kneeled in the drive to secure the cans well to the hitch. After giving the rope a good tug, Eva poked a hole through the wax paper lining each can. The cans wouldn't drag on the ground, but they would dangle very close to the road.

With each bump Eva hit on the way to the university over the next few weeks, the daily refilled cans slowly shook a little more of Nick's ashes onto the pavement.

With each nightly refill, Eva began to feel a bit lighter, even as the frequent swings thru drive-thrus, two or more a day, caused her dress to become increasingly tight around the waist.

While there were whispers in the halls, and it became clear to the Dean that some were even enraged, mainly those who never liked Eva in the first place, the Dean never said anything about Eva's attire. He assumed she was taking her time teaching *Great Expectations,* forgetting that Eva taught American literature, and he admired her ability to captivate the students so. He nodded approvingly in the halls. Julia also adjusted easily; she was used to giving her mother little thought.

While the gown seemed interminable to many, it really wasn't more than three weeks before neither Eva nor Julia could zip the back of Eva's dress at all. Eva was still wearing the cape every day, the warm temperatures had not yet arrived, and it helped to cover some of the stains and tears that had begun to appear on the dress, as well as the ever-widening zipper, but the gown simply wasn't comfortable anymore. Eva began to feel sewn in.

Eva removed the dress and the cans one night while Julia was at work, and filled another black trash bag, adding another lump to the bedroom floor.

Pills and Other Necessities

The kettle is whistling. I reach for our cups; I am making tea for Irma and me. Her mug is the one that reads: "I like poetry, long walks on the beach, and poking dead things with a stick." She bought it while we were on vacation and I can still hear the roar that escaped her lips in that campy Five-and-Dime. She had stood before me in her bathing suit, moist with sea water, a Hawaiian print skirt wrapped around her then very slender waist (I had marveled at her waist since I had never learned to tie anything around mine so that it would stay put and also because my own waist hadn't been that small since I was twelve), sand still dotting the tops of her feet, facing a rotating rack. Head back, wide mouthed, she had laughed while I watched her in profile. Then she had whipped her head around and flashed me a grin as she read the mug out loud with glee, grasping it in her hands with the sort of familiarity one has with a mug one has been drinking morning coffee from for years. That mug was hers before she had purchased it in the same way that I was hers before we had met.

My mug Irma had bought for me one holiday as a joke, and her jokes had a funny way of sticking. It was partly the way they were often based on truths that few were willing to admit, let alone say. Mine read: "Talk to the brains of this operation, she's right over there," and it had an arrow. Of course, since the mug was round it was hard to tell which way the arrow was pointing and it seemed to be pointing right back to the saying, which suggested that the person holding the mug ought to be a woman and that the mug owner was actually complimenting not diminishing herself. This is partly what Irma loved about it—she loved double entendres. Half the joy of everything came from double meanings, substitutions, and innuendo. In my case the mug meant that Irma's morning routine was to debate on which side of me she needed to sit in order for the mug to mean what she had intended. Some jokes never get old.

I pour the hot water over the chamomile bag in Irma's mug and the black tea bag in mine, and then I shuffle into the sunroom. My mug has three shots of Gosling's Old Rum waiting at the bottom. It is early, only 6 a.m., and the sun is just beginning to shine through the shady oaks behind our house. It is Sunday, our lazy day for tea drinking, leafing through the magazines and catalogs that stack up during the week, and reading from our regularly mounting piles of books that hold various bookmarks haphazardly poking this way and that. Irma's current stack includes a book of contemporary poetry; a physics and a DNA book for laypeople; *Breakfast at Tiffany's*—she loves the character Holly Golightly and rereads the book once every few years; *Cancer: 50 Essential Things to Do*; *How to Fight Cancer and Win*; *Beating Cancer with Nutrition*; *The Cure for All Cancers: Including over 100 Case Histories of Persons Cured*; and a complete collection of the poems of John Keats. The Keats' book tops the stack and is marked at his "This Living Hand," by one of her favorite headshots of me. The poem is speculated to be Keats' last, and possibly to have been written for Fanny Brawne, the woman with whom he was in love:

> This living hand, now warm and capable
> Of earnest grasping, would, if it were cold
> And in the icy silence of the tomb,
> So haunt thy days and chill thy dreaming nights
> That thou wouldst wish thine own heart dry of blood
> So in my veins red life might stream again,
> And thou be conscience-calmed—see here it is—
> I hold it towards you.

While in the poem the lover ought to wish to trade her life for his, as with everything else, Irma's interpretation held a slightly different twist.

To the left of Irma's book stack is mine, which includes various books on fly-fishing, philosophy, and history. On top of my stack is a new bookmark: Irma's laminated obituary which ran in the paper last Sunday, and which kindly arrived from the funeral home in yesterday's mail.

Images of Irma, me, and Irma and me adorn the white bookcases that lean against the south wall. They are held in various frames Irma decoupaged herself, carefully selecting from magazines, flyers, and advertisements images and words that she felt aptly and humorously described a particular scene. There is one of us, arms around each other's waists, on the beach in the Outer Banks. She decoupaged the frame with images of seashells, crabs, and other ocean life she had clipped, but she had also added the phrases "catches biggest fish," "great bass," "best crabs," and "eat here." Like Irma's mug, the phrases are connected to arrows that point waggishly this way and that.

When I first met Irma she was working in the library at my university. I'd see her behind the counter, long, straight, dark hair, bangs hanging in front of her big brown eyes. She was impish and shy. She'd always been scuttling around in the stacks, busying herself to intentionally avoid interaction. One day I was returning a stack of books late in the evening; I had been working in my office grading papers until about 10:30 and I carried some books over on my way home. As it was nearing 11:00, closing time, and it was a Thursday night, no students were studying and the library was empty. Irma was sitting uncharacteristically relaxed, feet up on a footstool reading Nietzsche's *The Gay Science*. She didn't see me come in and so I had the luxury of observing her, if only for a moment, completely at ease and un-self-conscious. When she saw me, she leapt to her feet, fumbled a bit, gestured toward the empty chairs and tables, and said apologetically that it had been "entirely dead" since about seven. I dismissed her concern with being found out and launched into inquiries about her interest in Nietzsche, what other books of his she had read, and if she could recall any favorite aphorisms. Her demeanor entirely changed. She became outspoken, gesturing wildly and speaking rapidly, only partly aware that I was her audience. From that moment on I was hooked. It soon became apparent she was, too.

When Irma got cancer we talked about how things would inevitably go. How she would decline, what we would do before that happened, what actions should follow her demise. Now I am sitting in our sunroom, numb, contemplating the next act of our play. To the right of my stack of books are the bottles, about thirty total. In the twenty-three years we were together, we kept a large Tupperware container on the top shelf of the closet, in the back, with the remainder pills for every prescription we had ever filled. The container includes painkillers and antibiotics for toothaches, urinary tract and kidney infections, severe headaches, sprained ankles, and the list goes on. The day Irma died, I added to the container the remainders of the litany of drugs they had tried on her until the very end, when the drugs were then administered simply to keep her out of her misery, and pills done away with in favor of a drip system that meant she didn't have to wait a moment for some inevitably overburdened nurse to administer the next morphine fix. If only I had that drip system, what I am about to do might be simpler.

By now the rum is having its fully desired effect. I stand and head to the kitchen to add another three shots to my mug. On an empty stomach, my head is foggy enough for the walk to the kitchen to be an experience in slow motion. I remove the tea bag and the fresh pour mixes with the residue at the bottom of my cup, only slightly watering down the taste of the Gosling. Standing at the kitchen counter, flashes of Irma flood my mind. At first I hear her laughter, see her dancing, smiling, and then there are the images of us making love, fast and furious, slow and intense, and then our wedding day, the birthday when I presented her with a trip to Paris, and then our last moments. I close my eyes, holding the counter fiercely, and try to resurrect her touch on my skin, the feel of her face on the tips of my fingers as I glide them across the surface of her cheek and down to her chin. I'm swaying my head back and forth deep in memory, attempting to summon the sensation of her lips touching mine. It's been a week and it seems like forever since I last held her. How can I summon those eyes, the intensity and depths of them? How can I bring them back, gaze into them, embrace her?

I remember how she had looked at me since that first conversation in the library. Her affection for me had never waned, and neither had mine for her. She could send messages through her gaze that were mutually understood, and I can clearly recall how she reminded me of our pact during the last day she was able to talk. Her voice was drowsy and stilted, the energy each word took evident in her concentration. "Adrian," she said, "You–don't live–without me—because—you—feel—you—must," she had said with deep determination, and with the sort of tone a mother might use when telling her child that just because the other kids are jumping off a bridge, he doesn't have to (though in characteristic Irma fashion her inference was the opposite). "You—meet me—on the—other—side." "You—re—memb—er—where—they—are—right?" "I know, top shelf, to the right of your winter sweaters. I haven't for-gotten," I had said.

Staring at the bottles, I take another swig from my mug. It is so quiet that I can hear myself swallow. The sun now warms the room and every glance about reminds me of her absence. Her mug is full, her books unmoved. Her afghan is tossed over the back of her chair, as though at any moment she is going to come in laughing about something, sit down, glance at me with that grin, pick up her mug, and begin chatting to me enthusiastically about what she finds so humorous. How many Sundays did we spend in this room? How many times did she come in just that way? Now it seems like so few, and yet they resonate so powerfully. How many days in a year? How many weeks? How many Sundays? How many years did we have this routine? It has all vanished so quickly, her scent is still fresh on the wool afghan. I reach over and pull it to me, ball it up, and bury my nose in a bunched section. Breathing deeply, I close my eyes and envision her.

Death will not unite us. I know that. We both knew that. There is no afterlife, and who would want one anyway? Why go on for an eternity as something not fully human? I want the feel of her skin, the touch of her lips, the smell of her. I don't want some ethereal vapor that I cannot even grasp. I want to be me and I want Irma to be her. I want this life, the life we knew together. An eternity spent not as myself and not with her as herself—that's a worse hell than living without her. What I want is the absence of pain, absence of grief, absence of absence. To wish for an absence of memory would be to undo all that came before—the beauty, the sadness, the joy, and the treasure of a life spent with Irma. I don't want another life with someone else. I don't want another life with her somewhere that is not here. I want to take what I have had, to savor it, rejoice in it, and to end with it in my arms. If I could wish for anything it would be eternal recurrence.

I begin unscrewing the caps of the bottles and dumping them out one by one. I want them mixed together. I don't want to know what I am ingesting, exactly. Precision isn't the point. An onslaught, that's what we had always hoped would do the trick. Part of me wants to be sober, to dump the contents of my mug down the drain, to face it and her with a full awareness of the act so that in my imagination I am fully there. But if I am going to do this right, do it as we had planned, then I need as many competing drugs in my system as possible. The anti-depressants I'd been prescribed since Irma's death (and which I haven't yet taken), the painkillers, the alcohol, and whatever else is in these bottles that I can't even begin to recall. Years of a life spent together are bottled up in these miscellaneous prescriptions for illnesses entirely forgotten. It's strange how time is spent. I have no capacity to remember why, exactly, Irma was prescribed amoxicillin, but there it is, clearly printed on a label with her name. I strain to recall an episode in 1998 when she would have been prescribed this drug, but I don't know. That's not what I know about Irma. What I know about Irma is how she affected me. What I know about Irma is what she became in the time we were together, how she learned to show everyone else those impish qualities I loved, how she went from being a shy woman behind a desk at the university library to standing totally unaware in that bathing suit in that Five-and-Dime, completely in herself, without any visibly apparent insecurity.

Irma had her insecurities, but in the time we had been together she had flowered into something unbelievable. She had just let more and more of herself out every day until everyone around us fell in love with the Irma I had been in love with since that first Thursday night.

Irma and I didn't tire of each other; we didn't want separation. It wasn't how we were made, at least not together. We realized early on that we didn't want children, if only because we knew they would need us and take us away from each other. We didn't want anything in between us. We had friends, but we socialized with them together. We had jobs, and we of course went to those independently, but every other waking minute was spent together. We thought about children a few times, but each time we were reminded of what it would really mean, forever. We also knew that if one of us should die, we would have to go on for the sake of the child or children, and that was not something either of us wanted to have to do. We knew that we wanted to live together and die together. We didn't want any forced separations, any body, any life, any thing to get between us.

We were together less than a year when we realized we would live together and die together, but we didn't yet know how to make it a reality. It was just something we both understood, and it was one of those understandings that we conveyed just by looking at each other whenever we watched a movie about a spouse or lover dying or whenever we read or heard about the same. All we had to do is glance at each other and we knew: that was never going to happen to us, not quite like that anyway. We knew we couldn't control how we would die or when, but we knew that, if we didn't die together in some sort of catastrophe, it wouldn't be long before we would find each other again, if only through release.

Then when we'd been together about five years, Irma came across a poem by Richard Cranshaw titled "Epitaph." I placed a copy of the poem beside the bottles last night before going to bed. Last night I listened to the music we loved, slept for the last time in our bed, and found that poem and copied it on our personal copier so that it would be here this morning for me to read again. I remember when Irma first discovered it. She brought it home and stood in the kitchen, reading it to me, her eyes filling with water and her voice unsteady:

> To these, whom Death again did wed,
> This grave's their second marriage-bed;
> For though the hand of Fate could force
> 'Twixt soul and body a divorce,

It could not sunder man and wife
Because they both lived but one life.

That was when we figured out how to do it.

Of course the poem isn't literal, we would never be buried together. Irma and I wanted to be cremated; Irma already has been. Her ashes are sitting in an urn to the right of my arm. I brought them home on Friday.

I had gotten things in order at the funeral home, done what they call "planning." I paid ahead for my cremation, wrote down what my wishes were. Sam, at the funeral home, had been very kind. He wasn't sure if I was ready to make such decisions, thought perhaps that I was rushing things, or maybe wanted to wait a few weeks or a month to go over such details since I had so recently handled the details of Irma's demise. I assured him now was the time. I explained that it offered me some comfort knowing that these details would be taken care of, and that, while we wouldn't be buried together, he would know what my wishes were: to have my ashes scattered in the same place Irma's had been. I told him a private ceremony for Irma was planned for a few weeks from now and that I would get the details to him shortly, and if he could please place them on file, he would know what my wishes were for my scattering.

Yesterday afternoon I drafted the letter to the funeral home explaining where Irma's ashes were to be scattered, along with my own. I hand wrote the letter so there would be no suspicion of foul play; I included a copy of my driver's license as verification for the signature. I sent the letter certified. It would arrive on Monday, tomorrow.

Irma and I had spent many lovely afternoons in a nearby park sunning and reading by the lake. It reminded Irma of the English Lake country, the home of the English Lake poets. We would pack a picnic, share a bottle of wine, read, and learn about botany and insects together. Those afternoons had always been exclusively about us. Hardly anyone made use of that area. The park was large and most people stayed in the areas by the playgrounds, campgrounds, grills, or the large lake where there was fishing, boating, and skiing. It was a bit of a hike to get to this little lake, and there were no activities to be had on it. There were no bathrooms nearby, no playgrounds, no people. It was our quiet place where we escaped the world and retreated into what made us us. We found solace in our togetherness in the peaceful quiet of that place. That was where we would be scattered, together.

The rum is starting to wear off. It is nearing 11:00 a.m. I get up to get the Gosling bottle, and this time pour a mug full. It is past teatime. I don't typically drink Gosling, it's an expensive rum, but I bought it for this special occasion. I want to celebrate.

I return to the sunroom with the bottle of Gosling and a 2-liter bottle of water. I top off the tea in Irma's mug with a little Gosling—we clink mugs, or at least I clink our mugs.

I stare at the dumped pills from the bottles. There are a lot of them. I'm hoping I can take them all. When I was a kid I had trouble taking pills. At first my mom had crushed them up in sugar water, then she had made me practice by swallowing M&M's. Irma was worried about that, but she had us both practice every day by taking a multitude of daily vitamins. When the healthy practice began it was so we could both live forever, and also because we didn't yet know which one of us would go first, so we both had to practice swallowing those pills.

I organize the pills from small to large. I figure I should start with the large ones, just in case I begin having difficulty swallowing. That's what Irma, in the end, had suggested. Another swig from my mug, and the play begins.

I walk to the filing cabinet and get out my Will; then I walk to the bookcase and take down Nietzsche's *The Gay Science*; then I go to the stereo and cue up one of our favorite CDs: Queen's Greatest Hits I & II. Some of the songs are long, and I am hoping that by the time the music stops, I will have too. I carry my Will, Nietzsche, and the remote back to the couch. I place the Will on the table. Opening the book, I take a straight swig of the Gosling and read aloud *On the Last Hour*, aphorism 315: "Storms are my danger. Will I have my storm of which I will perish, as Oliver Cromwell perished of his storm? Or will I go out like a light that no wind blows out but that becomes tired and sated with itself—a burned-out light? Or finally: will I blow myself out lest I burn out?"

I sit back on the couch, place Irma's afghan over me, and hit play on the remote. I listen to track nine on disk two first, "Who Wants to Live Forever?" Then I begin to rhythmically swallow pills in beats to the music, "…who wants to live forever, when love must die…," alternating between the Gosling and the water.

I am thinking about the Keats' poem and extending my hand toward Irma. I am imagining her joking with me about wanting more than my hand, as she would, if she were here (and she is), certainly play on the synecdochical image of only my hand reuniting with her.

As I swallow, drink, and sway to the music, I become more and more sleepy, woozy, foggy-headed.

I take a last look at the prescription bottles, and as I close my eyes, I imagine Irma sitting beside me, head cocked to the side, saying with an impish grin on her face and that knowing look in her eyes:

"There are some things that can't be prescribed."

There Once Was a Man Who Thought Too Much

There once was a man who thought too much
thought too much thought too much.
He lived on an island in the borough of
wee wah wah and slept not at all.
His back was strong his legs were long and
he wore a moustache below his nose—
and fur one supposes upon his chin.
It all started when he was just a boy
and was dreaming about it.
About what he was dreaming is what
we do not entirely know
but it had something to do with what
is what and what was what
and so he went and found a book and
then he sat within a crook
and as he turned the pages of that book he
began to think and think about it.
As he read and thought and read and thought he
wondered what if anything others thought

so he took that book and gathered some more and
went from his crook to a crescent on a hill
where others who also began as boys left as men
and he not only thought and thought
about it more than others seemed to but he
somehow some way on many a day
began to teach other girls and boys to think about it too.
One day when all the books were put away and
he was thinking thinking about what he had
done and what he would do and how to give
to others all the thought he ever knew
his thinking grew and grew.
This man who thought too much thought
too much thought too much
first saw a thinning in his hair. His eyes
squinted to procure what was not there
but all he saw was that part in his hair. So he
thought and thought and thought about it
and then he washed what was not there with
little care and left the rest to bear.
On another day while walking down a summer
lane he thought he saw a willow in the air,
taking the willow as just as fair as what
was departing from his hair
he grasped it between thumb and forefinger
and put it in the part that was there.
The willow blew and blew about leaving his part
without and as he chased it down the lane
his legs that were too long seemed to disintegrate in thin air!
With each stride his part widened and his gait spasmed

and soon it was as though his legs were
not there—he was gliding on air!
The man who thought and thought
about the thinning in his hair
was now losing his legs his only pair. This
he thought was quite rare.
With himself down to his legs that were not there
and with that part dividing wider his thinning hair
he began to think and think and think
about what had gone awry
for before he had always seemed quite spry.
Strong back strong legs and fur beneath
his nose one had never supposed
his grasp between thumb and forefinger
would no longer grip what was there
but would somehow lead him to what was not.
The book's leaves that he would leaf when
he was loafing in the summer breeze
upon that hill that he could no longer climb
had the answer he was trying to find.
As he reached for another book to see what others thought
and determine what had somehow
brought what had been brought
upon him to others too his grip gave way to another waylay—
his arms had grown taut.
Not for naught but first it was the thinning of his hair
and then the legs that were no longer there
and now the arms had grown thin, taut
and about this he thought and thought.
The more he thought the more he read and
the more he read the more he learned

it was not the thinning in his hair that had led to this despair
but the loss of strength in his legs his only pair
and his arms which now no longer felt there.
Before he knew it his lips would cease moving
and air that had always been without a care
would be heaving—it would be entirely rare and unfair.
Those who knew not what to do made absent queries:
Had this to do with the thinning in his hair?
Had his hair to do with the thinking that had been?
What happened to the legs no longer there?
What about that willow placed in his hair?
No, no nothing is so unfair that it
punishes those who think so fair
yet somehow the thinking that had had
such a good run caused people
to start to point and stare not at the thinning in his hair
but at the thinning of what was still there.
Unmoving the rest were moved as he thought
and thought and thought about it.
While he could not bring back the legs no longer there
or the arms in need of repair and while
his lips only gently passed air
his thinking thinking thinking taught and
taught and taught all about it.
Like the other boys and girls who glide on air
because the body they once had is no longer there
it was not because of thought that life
brought too much to bear.
The man who thought too much had not
used up all his thinking—those fools!
There are no such rules.

But if we do as the man had done and
we think and think and think
until our own days are done we may too go
taut (or not) but not for naught—
we will have taught others not only
how to live but how to die,
and through thought we may even try
and write down for others to read how to survive
not only the loss of this man and other
boys girls and women like him
but we may devise a plan for how to undo
what his thinking had not done
but with more thinking what could have been done.
If we can do this we will somehow have won.

Publishing Credits

"The thing is" first appeared in *Eunoia Review*

"Trespassing" first appeared in *Connotation Press*

"By Sweater" first appeared in *Grey Sparrow Press*

"Yo-Yo" first appeared in *Connotation Press*

"He Undertook Her" first appeared in *Bartleby Snopes*

"Rotary Dial" first appeared in *Every Day Fiction*

"The Grief Eater" first appeared in *Picayun*e and was reprinted in *Easy Street*

"Dressing the Part" first appeared in *Adelaide*

"Pills and Other Necessities" first appeared in *Down in the Dirt*

"There Once Was a Man Who Thought Too Much" first appeared in *Beorh Quarterly*

About the Author

Deirdre Fagan is a widow, wife, and mother of two who writes poetry, fiction, creative nonfiction, and essays on literary criticism and pedagogy. She is the author of the book Critical Companion to Robert Frost, and the articles, "Kay Ryan and Poetic Play," published in the CEA Critic, and "Emily Dickinson's Unutterable Word," collected in Bloom's Modern Critical Views: Emily Dickinson, among others. Her academic and creative work is available in various online and print journals, magazines, and anthologies. Fagan's poem, "Outside In," was a finalist for Best of the Net 2018, and her poem, "Homesick," was nominated for a 2018 Pushcart. She has a poetry chapbook, Have Love, from Finishing Line Press (2019).

Fagan is a native New Yorker who has previously lived in Arizona, Florida, Illinois, and Maryland. She currently resides in Michigan where she is associate professor and coordinator of creative writing in the English, Literature, and World Languages Department at Ferris State University. Fagan coordinates the Literature in Person series, which brings national and regional authors to Ferris, and facilitates National Poetry Month events celebrating the genre through poetry readings, discussions, and activities. Fagan teaches creative writing, composition, poetry, and American literature. Meet her at deirdrefagan.com.